THE BOY WHO SWALLOWED A
RAINBOW

WRITTEN AND ILLUSTRATED BY TREVOR ROMAIN

BOYDS MILLS PRESS

Text and illustrations copyright © 1993 by Trevor Romain
All rights reserved

Published by Caroline House
Boyds Mills Press, Inc.
A Highlights Company
815 Church Street
Honesdale, Pennsylvania 18431
Printed in China

U.S. Cataloging-in-Publication Data
   (Library of Congress Standards)

Romain, Trevor.
    The boy who swallowed a rainbow / written and illustrated by
Trevor Romain.
[32]p. : col. ill. ; cm.
Originally published: Bright Books, 1993.
Summary: When a young boy becomes famous for swallowing a rainbow, he
discovers being a celebrity is not as fun as he thought it would be.
ISBN 1-56397-920-9
1. Rainbow — Fiction. 2. Publicity — Fiction. I. Title.
   [E] 21 2000   AC   CIP
00-100346

First Boyds Mills Press edition, 2000
The text of this book is set in 16-point Times.

10 9 8 7 6 5 4 3 2 1

In loving memory of my father, Jac,
who brought so much color into my life.

"I don't like living on a farm," said Lucas, even though he was surrounded by fresh air, fresh water, lots of animals and at least fifty-five types of insects.

He sat on top of his favorite hill and sulked. "I'm bored," he said. "I'm definitely bored."

Although there was plenty to do, like milking the cows, feeding the African fainting goats and watering the miniature pigs, Lucas moped around the farm. He was looking for attention, but no one paid much notice to him. The cows kept on chewing, the bugs kept on bugging, the insects kept on insecting and the sheep kept on following each other around and never going anywhere.

"Dumb sheep," he muttered. Then he said, "I wish I could be famous like people on television. That would stop me from being bored. I know it would."

"I've got it!" said Lucas. "If I grow the biggest pumpkin in the world, I'm sure I'll be famous." He pictured himself standing next to a giant pumpkin six feet tall, having his picture taken for the cover of *Time* magazine.

Lucas knew he was on to something. So he quickly planted a pumpkin seed in the ground. He watered it well and watched it grow—for about two minutes. Then he stood up and spoke to the little mound on the ground. "Please grow," he said. "Please, please, please." But the pumpkin didn't grow. He tried again. "Please grow. Please, please . . . PUH-LEASE!" But the pumpkin still didn't grow and Lucas was bored again.

It happened at two forty-three the following afternoon. Purely by chance and completely by mistake, Lucas yawned and accidentally swallowed a rainbow that just HAPPENED to be above his head at the time. GULP!

Lucas was amazed. Every time he spoke, bubbles of colored sentences escaped from his mouth. BLURP.
He said to his friend Sabina, "I feel so weird. BLURP."

"Beautiful," said Sabina, holding up a mirror. "Absolutely beautiful."

"Why thank you . . . BLURP . . ." said Lucas, blushing. "I think you're beautiful, too. BLURP."

"Not you," said Sabina. "The colors coming out of your mouth are beautiful. You're just a pinhead."

Lucas didn't really care what Sabina thought anyway, because before he could BLURP many more BLURPS, he became rather famous.
And not at all bored.

In no time at all he did 412 television appearances, 208 radio interviews, 106 talk shows, 97 benefits, 75 gala events, 29 television commercials and answered at least 2 million stupid questions.

Lucas gave colorful speeches all over the country. People came from far and wide, up and down and even sideways to hear him.

Lucas thought he liked being famous, but he really didn't. He hated people patting him on the head and messing up his hair, which took him ages to gel.

He hated very large ladies with lots of lipstick who said very loudly, "ISN'T HE A DARLING? BRING ME THAT LITTLE CHEEK OF YOURS," and they'd pinch his cheeks and tweak his nose.

He hated sleeping in hard hotel beds with no patchwork quilts.

He hated other people telling him what to do, where to go and when to blow his nose.

He hated being pushed and pulled so much, that some days he wished he were alone on the farm with absolutely nothing to do, except milk the cows, feed the African fainting goats and water the miniature pigs.

Then everything changed.

B eing famous makes you noticed by all sorts of strange people. People you normally wouldn't associate with.

One day, while the security guard was having a quick nap on the job, Lucas was snatched away by two men and taken to a secret hideaway. "What do you want?" yelled Lucas.

The men said, "We want the pot of gold at the end of that rainbow you swallowed."

"There's no gold inside me," said Lucas. "If there were, I'd weigh 900 pounds and my stomach would rest on my ankles."

"We read about it in a book," said one of the men.

"BUT THAT'S JUST A DUMB KID'S STORY!" yelled Lucas.

"So," said one of the men. "You're just a dumb kid. Open him up, Fred."

"Err . . . no, you open him up, Ned."

"No way, you open him up, Fred."

"But I can't stand the sight of blood," said Fred.

"Neither can I," said Ned.

"I've got it," said Fred.

"Got what?" asked Ned.

"An idea," said Fred.

"Where did you get it?" asked Ned.

"From a book," said Fred. "We'll lock him in a giant supermarket refrigerator. Then he'll catch a cold and SNEEZE up all the gold coins."

"Great idea," said Ned.

So they locked Lucas in the refrigerator and set the temperature on Extremely Cold.

Lucas got colder and colder and angrier and angrier and instead of catching a cold, Lucas caught his breath and yelled at the top of his voice. "GET ME OUT OF HERE; THE GEL IN MY HAIR IS FREEZING AND IT FEELS WEIRD!"

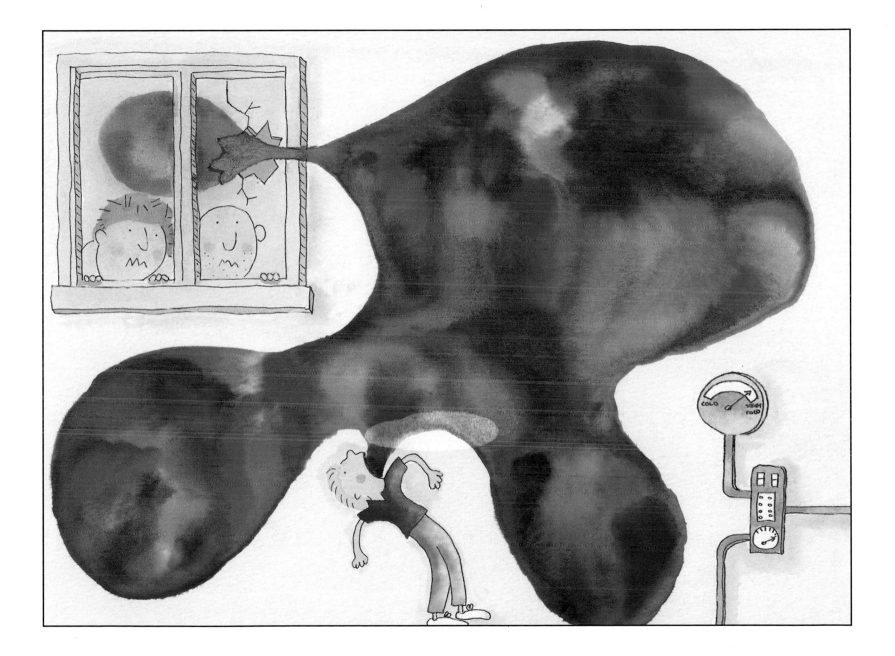

Lucas shouted so loudly that the men unlocked the door and ran away. And the rainbow escaped from his mouth and attached itself to the icicles hanging in the refrigerator. (They were later removed and sold as popsicles.)

Without the rainbow to make him famous, Lucas soon became unfamous. (Although he still does some guest appearances for the Great American Popsicle Company.)

People stopped asking him for autographs, and photographers stopped hiding in the bushes on the farm. "I think I prefer living a NORMAL boring life," said Lucas, "on a NORMAL farm, with all the NORMAL animals . . .

and all my NORMAL friends doing what they NORMALLY do.
Like Sabina trying to break every bone in Malcolm's body. That's pretty
NORMAL for Sabina. Kim trying to hold his breath under water while
tap dancing. That's pretty NORMAL for Kim. And Bobby trying to turn
the cat into a musical instrument. That's pretty NORMAL for Bobby."

Lucas still lives on the farm and often gets bored, but he's learned to live with it. When he goes up to his special place on the hill to think about his future and reflect upon his past, he NEVER yawns without covering his mouth. (And by the way, he's stopped using gel in his hair. He prefers the NORMAL look.)